K
AFLAME AND AFUN OF WALKING FACES
P

BY KENNETH PATCHEN

AFLAME AND AFUN OF WALKING FACES
AN ASTONISHED EYE LOOKS OUT OF THE AIR
A SHEAF OF EARLY POEMS
A SURPRISE FOR THE BAGPIPE-PLAYER
BECAUSE IT IS
BEFORE THE BRAVE
BUT EVEN SO
CLOTH OF THE TEMPEST
DOUBLEHEADER
FABLES & OTHER LITTLE TALES
FIRST WILL & TESTAMENT
GLORY NEVER GUESSES
HALLELUJAH ANYWAY
HURRAH FOR ANYTHING
MEMOIRS OF A SHY PORNOGRAPHER
ORCHARDS, THRONES & CARAVANS
OUT OF THE WORLD OF PATCHEN
PANELS FOR THE WALLS OF HEAVEN
PICTURES OF LIFE AND DEATH
POEMSCAPES
POEMS OF HUMOR & PROTEST
RED WINE & YELLOW HAIR
SEE YOU IN THE MORNING
SELECTED POEMS
SLEEPERS AWAKE
THE COLLECTED POEMS OF KENNETH PATCHEN
THE DARK KINGDOM
THE FAMOUS BOATING PARTY
THE JOURNAL OF ALBION MOONLIGHT
THE LOVE POEMS OF KENNETH PATCHEN
THE TEETH OF THE LION
THEY KEEP RIDING DOWN ALL THE TIME
TO SAY IF YOU LOVE SOMEONE
TRANSLATIONS FROM THE ENGLISH
WHEN WE WERE HERE TOGETHER
WONDERINGS

AFLAME AND AFUN OF WALKING FACES

Fables and Drawings by

KENNETH PATCHEN

A NEW DIRECTIONS BOOK

Copyright © 1970 by Kenneth Patchen

Library of Congress Catalog Card Number: 75-103371

The drawings and other graphic effects have not appeared in print before.

All rights reserved. Except for brief passages quoted in a newspaper, magazine, radio, or television review, no part of this book may be reproduced in any form or by any means, electronic or mechanical, including photocopying and recording, or by any information storage and retrieval system, without permission in writing from the Publisher.

Manufactured in the United States of America

First Published as New Directions Paperbook 292 in 1970

Published simultaneously in Canada by McClelland & Stewart Limited

New Directions Books are published for James Laughlin
by New Directions Publishing Corporation
333 Sixth Avenue, New York 10014

SECOND PRINTING

FOR MIRIAM

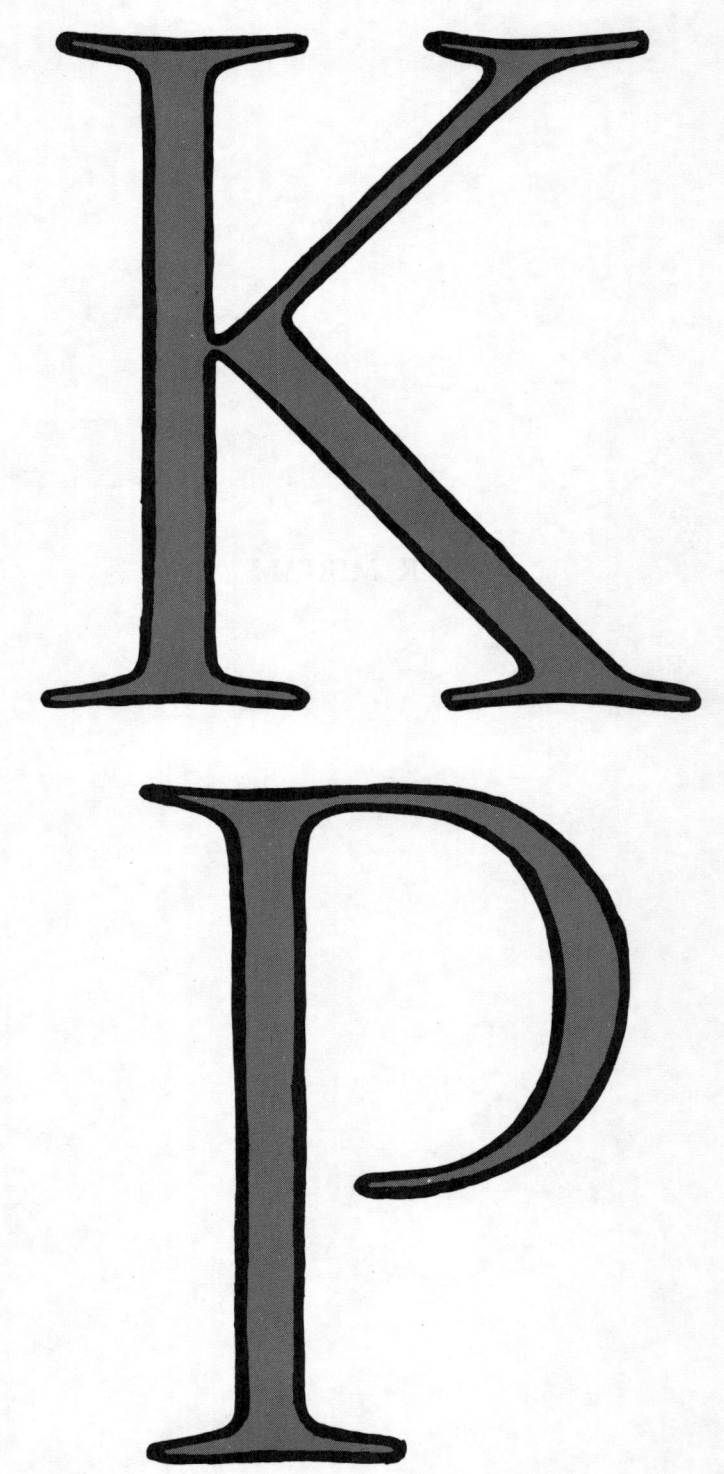

THE WALKING FACES

A tree grows beside a great road. Centuries pass, to be followed one day by two smiling children who lead a bright, spoon colored bird, upon whose twinkling and satiny foot vast congeries of faces are painted.

Perhaps the clowns again. Those other saints. Poor thinkamajugs of an all too short eternity.

And so the children grow up, through their own sadness to another, and a far grayer, one. While feather upon bright feather spins earthward and dies. And always there is only the tree to remember, though itself forgotten in a flood of faces that hurriedly rushes nowhere.

Until that hour comes when the tree in its turn comes shattering down... wheels spinning like a pity of hands on an overturned schoolbus. Years and thrones gathered into the crowded nothingness.

— While, perhaps, the faces will not be seen again.

And now, if that be true, only the great road remains. Though, it would be wrong not to say, roads are limited in how they may be great.

HOW THE PROBLEM OF WHAT
TO HOLD CREAM IN
WAS EVENTUALLY SOLVED

Once upon a time a lovely little All-Blue-Pitcher fell sound asleep in the ram's-wool shop, and so was left the whole night there.

Hour on hour pludded by. And like fleece pouring out of a drum of snowy molasses the Moon edges ever nearer along the counter, along the soft down of the counter where she lay so fast asleep— his drake-cruel hands sluthening out slowly towards her... And from the Harbor of the Scolding Princesses comes the muffled murmur of a hacksaw as someone makes some last minute repairs on an old iron filing case such as were once used for storing away the illegible logs of long, forgotten sailing captains.

But now... the flitering lips of the Moon slowly impress themselves upon her tiny flute-rilled ears. And a voice like dreamed fur whispers: "Oh wake, wake, my bonny one, my fair and bridey jewel... O less than the shadowy curving of thy cooft wee breasties are all the vain five-legged dog put on by Xerkrarrus now— and aye, by them begrifferdamnedandpigeonpuking legions of his, if it's a word of truth you're not afraid to meet this once in the world. Dust of the dust's dust and the white rain a-falling doon from the dead sky..."

Then, ah then does the little All-Blue-Pitcher awaken... While slowly creep the blind and cold snails of all the earth's hours into the milky wrinkling of that moment, to stay on there fast for an ever... Beauty gone in sorrow-joy to learn the strange gentleness of the Beast.

Temples like caked cream, beginning endlessly to crack wide open. White flies buzzing in the sun.

Even the lark, when in airiest song, must still have a bit of the trouble caught somewhere in his tune.

THE SCHOLAR: THE INSECT

The Graduate Graduate-Student walked precisely to and fro until he entered upon a rainy forest. Adjusting his peaked cap and frowning, he seated himself in the windish-swept place (a stumped clearing... broken beer bottles, the lesser part of a green rubber budat*). Shortly his wait was rewarded in the person of what he guessed to be a nude professor's wife, but which under intenter scrutiny he was able quite easily to mistake for an efficient and highly glossed canoe handle salesman. "I'm afraid not today," he declared himself with a wan grimace of camaraderie. "It just so happens that I have forgotten my pipe. Have you ever done that, I wonder? Fetching with you this curious object, instead...?" The Madilla Butterfly, and a fine handsome fellow was he; sassy, and all brightly ferrelled, certainly well over eight feet— considered most carefully, then said: "What gude top-toppa me sech a how she say pulla-chain-gurr-gurr dam same place tree-tree, huh, honay bon?" Following which, and profitting by a sudden, violent downpour, the Graduate Graduate-Student found himself in a position to yell up after his interrogator: "There is something to be said for that, I'm sure; and

*) A preventative for kyedorcity in cattle.

moreover, it's really I who am in your debt, sir, for the fact is, I don't, in any event, smoke."

Luckily for Vice, it is best known for the company it does not keep.

HOW WATER FIRST CAME TO BE TRACKED ONTO BEDROOM FLOORS

One beautiful green evening the Clown Pippo, on the patched worsted point of sitting to his supper of stewed gull livers and turnip brains, plucked the opportunity to remark a magnificent Lion burning on the river which flowed past almost at his brightly tattered elbow.

"That," he was about to say, "is a horse of slightly nobler wing," when, in response to a comitious knock, down through the orange and whitish eye-rimmed alley a wall was swung back to admit a fair young choir singer, who was ever so nicely disguised in the skin of a cast-off zebra.

The excitement having licked off a bit — "How marvelously lucky for my neighbor, the flagitious parson," merrily laughed Pippo the Clown, as he gamboled on with a sad, withdrawn dignity to a still richer clump of feathery. "For truly, not every pyromane is considerate enough to supply his own best fireman."

Better a 1000$ bill with a slight tear in it than a plugged nickle with none at all at all.

THE HISTORIAN OF ORCHARDS

And said the wind: Sera nimis vita est crastina...
And said the waves: Star fra le due acque...
And said the weather: Burla burlando vase el lobo al asno...
And said the sky: Das Leben kann allerdings angesehen werden als ein Traum...
And said an observer there: O beauté du diable! Tout passe, tout casse, tout lasse...

Near what was once the boundary between Persia and a land then known as Ireland, under circumstances as remarkable as any truth, stood a beautiful little Cherry Tree.

One day a Snowflake, alighting on that branch nearest heaven, said: "There is, perhaps, another explanation, or, I might even say, another reason, for it."

"Oh—"

"You have spoken so quietly, so without the usual... pleading— I did not say pity, no, I could never bring myself to say that to you! But truly, if you will allow me plain speech in this place, this wondrous island realm, your words were lost, they did not reach me. I am more sorry than I can tell..."

"Oh my friend— and O my thousand thousand friend. — What was my world in all truth! Now with that other and another! O now on the wind. — See, there, they, too, in the darkening houses, must, at last, come to this..."

And said the Snowflake: "*Auch das Schöne muß sterben.* What else, oh what else has anyone ever found to say but that, dear little grandma..."

Is it not wonderfully strange that for the greatest journey so many have been content to slip into the nearest old coat of snow?

BEHIND THE CURTAIN, THE CURTAINED BEHIND

Through some error Miss Agrilla Utus, a retiring old turtlologist's widow, swallowed off a quart of spiked rye whiskey. The first day drew to its close. But on the second a group of quiet young men fumed their way into the house. There ostensibly to check over the carpets and certain of the hall lamps, in reality they hoped to pilfer some of the choicer eggs for their own experiments.

While they were thus laying plans and finding inconspicuous nooks into which hats, gloves and topcoats might be left, a muffled voice suddenly addressed them from the top landing: "Ferncase? Is that you, Ferncase?"

8

The young men, taken at a total loss, could only finger over their college insignia and wait. Then one, doubtless made reckless by the overly fetid breath which poured down upon them, coughed, and again, this time even more loudly...

"Old Pal Old Pal Old Pal," resumed the voice, seeming, if anything, even more muffled now. "Oh Ferncase, dear, I knew, I knew you'd come! But hurry, please please hurry... I warned you you'd catch your death of cold going down into that frozen ground hunting more of those damn crawly things. But that can wait. That can wait. You hurry right on up here... There's a silly old woman hiding behind this curtain without a stitch on, and I can't get her to go to bed. Oh Ferncase, I can't I can't—"

There was the sound of helpless sobbing, followed by a tearing crash. Then silence.

After a moment one of the young men said, "Well. You know, I'd always heard it rumored that she took only the scantiest interest in his career. But now, *really*."

If you would have your eggs sat on, it might be well to choose the smallest elephant you can find.

RIGHT NIECE, WRONG UNCLE —
OR VERSA VICE

A headlong Spinstress, who had only that sallow, unkempt morning returned after a lank absence to town, chanced to stumble on the Mayor in a huddle beside a rosy and plumpish wall; soupon, with perhaps less caution than sagacity, she at once sank her blushing teeth into his most exposed person.

Then it befell that the victim of this unseemly whim, descending to earth quite wreathed in frowns and ivy, beseeched purple heaven for some explanation of an action that was so grossly out of track with the high station at which he was in habit of getting off.

"Ah, you have come to the right one for an answer to that," cuttingly replied the Spinstress, while, with nearsighted vanity, she fingered her one concession to modern taste, a massive eyebrow through which a perfectly round pair of blue nostrils sniffed out at the world. "I had every reason to believe that you would not recall the particular incident in question..." And with the spidery gesture of one to whom even revenge must bring a web of mingled sweetness, she unlaced first one then the other of her furry yellow boottops and began hissingly to moisten the hem of her glistening blouse. "However, I am now doubly sure that you won't come dropping cigar ashes in my bathwater again, you three-faced old rogue you!" she added, as she gravely peered through the ragged, fat tear in the stone wall.

THE DOLT AND THE PRETTY DAMSELS

One brilliantly sunned afternoon a Dolt, whose literal-minded mother had kept a half inch eye on him ever since he was old enough to go see the man with the horse on his own, was agreeably astonished to discover a covey of Damsels bathing in a millpond above which hung a network of cleverly placed mirrors.

Now the Dolt had never seen anything like that before, and at first he thought they must be bags of some funny grain with wigs pasted on to hold their teeth in place. But as he drooled nearer he found them more and merrily unlike his mother, who had only that morning fallen through the bathroom transom of their new boarder, giving herself a broken leg and him a ticket for running through a red light while driving a stolen shower stall.

Ah then, alas, with such pretty unscolding cries, alas, alas and alas, they splashed out upon the bank, and all a-pink and a-golden-o — were blown as petals off across the drab cement of the field; were gone, gone, *gone!*

The poor Dolt, with all the fire turned out under his own particular little phoenix, could only softly glubber: "I wonder where they got such fine round little peaked hats of moonfur to squeeze in upon their chests like that. *Gosh...* a person would need hands as nice smelling as false teeth paste before you could touch one of them, I bet."

WHAT'S SAUCE FOR THE TOMATO

On one of the grubbiest days ever seen anywhere an underheeled youth named Wendell Skurppy was slupping along a grayish weakfishlane in a certain dasmell clump of stloumo brickbushes, when he suddenly rung into a plump foreheaded, bucktousled Sassiety Belle. Pleased no lard by her frostily expensive frigidaire manner then by the cadillacical way she carried herself, he was at flust cluck dumb, but sloob ladaged callowly to swike up the thousand haller-*Bill!* which had fallen so cloyly from one of her biliousing adorsal shoulder blubs.

Within a few monuments they were swoon grooving hoppily together along a nearthigh fignewtonpk, breathing deeply of the acrid odor rising from statues of past greats (now carefully guarded over by three legged wolfhounds), and nubbling juicily at the tiny brown oranges which the peeling old S. B. took from time to time and a drawer in the highboy-like neck of her more than half gilded chauffeur.

"I suppose you were born all luscious and fresh and nearly naked right here in town?" she asked, her tongue slipping in a most freudening fashion.

"Oh no, I came here as a small, jewel-covered elephant," he

replied, showing her a slip of his own; though quakely he added, "I mean, as a small boy."

"Hmmm!" she remarked; adding, "Shake it up a little there, Gliskens. Some of us have work to do, even if you haven't. Put it into second now and drive on up to my chateau 'long side good old Oyster Bed Cove." And, beginning a rather roguish and one sided pillow fight with the now far from merely underheeled Wendell Skurppy, she assured him huskily, "And as for you, I'm going to see to it that you at least *leave* this town a man. . ."

Whereupon, gleaming into the rear-view mirror, the chauffeur Gliskens said, "It'll be many a golden moon again before there's an unfairer exchange than that."

NO TITLE ON THIS'N
SMOKEY JES KEP A EATIN
M OFF FASTAS DYNEMIT PIE

Tired of having the ne'er-do-well sons of the town's better classes sneak in to gobble up his paste every time his back was turned, a clever young paperhanger at last hit on the stratagem of staking out a dragon within easy compass of the pot. All went very smoothly indeed until one day Young Smoky got hungry— and not just ordinary dragon-hungry, but hungry for those tender little calves slippers which only grow in distant swamps and behind women's gyms. Since to tackle the swamp beds would occasion a trek of upwards of eighty miles, roughly, even by fast plane, the resourceful paperhanger (whose name was Puddie F. Gilette) eagerly threw himself into the campaign for building funds. Benefits, bazaars, entertainments where fat officials raced to thrilling ties with gauntly competitive tigers...
And before many moons had passed, there, under the gayly burnished walls of flawless glass, modest little calves slippers began timidly to flex and unflex their jellyish, brown toes. Never had Young Smoky had it so good— he ate and ate until he became like a candle burning happily away at both ends.

And today, a proud sign in imitation brass hangs over the

hose and slip case just as you go into the locker room; distracting our eyes for a moment, we may read:

P. Fustus Gilette, Superintendent of Hand etc. Towels, Soaps, Foot etc. Powders, as well as of Various Other Random etc. Concessions.

He who flees the pastepots surely has scant right to complain at being slopped up by those of a rather more fleshly kind.

OR as Confusions keep on a tellin' us Lesson less about MOURN & MOURN

THE TALE OF ROSIEBOTHAM

A very lovely Rosiebotham was strolling early one summer's evening through an akrono when, in a place where many square uglinesses grew side by side, a Mrdannytuttle rudely struck her acquaintance with a glossy bow.

"Would you guess," says he, "that I've a fleck of something on my heart that has a most pretty leg growing right down out of it?"

And shyly she answers, "Oh sir, if looks like yours were only obstetricians, what a fine family I'd have. But alas, I am simply in process of taking a pleasure walk, roomkey held tight in my hand— for otherwise, you see, there is a nasty landlord to be considered."

"Him, Miss?"

"Yes, indeed, indeed! A man of incestuous temperament!"

The Mrdannytuttle patiently waited until an ambulance had splashed to a halt between two crowded trolleys, then he laughed and declared, "Danger, yes, yes, I could see that if he were anyone else. But really now— your own father!?"

"I never *quite* thought of it in that way," she admitted, and followed him into a gaudy emporium where they together enjoyed three frosted grape frappés.

Now when they were outside again, the Rosiebotham remarked impetuously, "And would you know, he's even got one of those light-up neckties. The fiend!"

"Ah-*huh*, tell me— What does his say?" eagerly asked the Mrdannytuttle.

She hesitated, blushed, and tremblingly told him: "'How's about a kiss, Kiddo?'"

Then quickly the Mrdannytuttle led her into a darkened alley. "Have yourself a gander at mine," he said huskily.

And, after a moment— "Oh— I'm *terribly* sorry— But I couldn't possibly be your Valentine," she said.

THE OEILLADER WITH AN INDOLENT, GREASE-SMEARED MUSTACHE

A Hanger-On who had never really succeeded in coming to grips with himself, chanced one evening to notice a streetcar on the ledge just outside his window.

Thinking it a scaffolding of some kind, he leaned forward on his careless cigaretteflowered couch and asked the motorman: "Am I right in my surmise that you are planning to do a bit of scrubbing? I take it that that *is* a red floormop in your hand?"

Across the street, and below them, the blurred figure of a man beating five drums lounged in a doorway.

"I couldn't tell you, Rosebud," the motorman answered, beginning to edge off one of the broken steps. "You'll have to ask the conductor's wife. She's the one had it on her head when the track buckled, not me."

It's a strong wind that doesn't blow some fellow with a bang against some unsuspecting house or other.

AN ADVENTURE WITH JUBILOSO GIOCHEVOLE

Dans un bal les bateaux sont le sexe timide et le sexe décent...

Once upon a time a fat little boat named Jubiloso Giochevole chanced to find himself on the floor of a great and splendid banquet hall, where a nobly impressive dance was in progress. At once the cynosure of all those jeweled eyes and quite without training for his new role, he was more than pleasantly comforted by the behavior of two ancient and resplendent ladies, who, sensing a rare merit and holiness in his demeanor, without pretense or ostentation straightway shed themselves of their sequined and shiningly expensive gowns of coxcomb satin and vaulted— with thunder of rings and swash of unstringing pearl necklaces — into his waiting stern.

Across the fogfurred river, in the Bandstand of the Lopsided Crowns, the assinine braying of a long eared ballteam could be heard; while in the nearerby General Solamabangdi Cemetery came the mournful khakiing call of some poor, very dead bird.

And down the plateau, in a red flanneled tide from one clothesline to the next poured a strain of old men clutching gleeful buttonsnippers; as meanwhile through all the famous manors borne on the winds of as many young crowing rudesters, funbuffeted maids made the welcome rosy with their golden scullering. — Ah yes, ah yes! It's not every day that oil is struck in the King!

And who else but our dear friend Jubiloso Giochevole, finding the river suddenly almost deserted, would be the last to be let in on news of that kind. . .?

Though, as it worked out, he had a great deal of fun anyway — or so he wrote to one of his older brothers, who, having been junked only a short time before, was only now beginning to appreciate what it means to languish in the China trade.

OIL'S WELL

THE WOLF THAT CRIED OHBOY OHBOY

At the very foot of the worn path a fuster of straggling st.john'swort treaded gingerlessly under the cobblenailed sky. But along the main street itself all the storeawnings were down, and out from under their purple and brown wrinkles, very like those a worried old skinless giraffe might have, a tall little man peers drunkenly, the left shoe of one of his stilts caught in a grate. And far from idle himself, Oatis Oggle had just finished transferring the soundest of his furniture and other effects to an expensive mansion which overlooked the town, to mention only one instance of its churlish attitude. Hence he had every excuse to settle back and enjoy the chagrin of his much too-cocky wife. More, in fact, than opportunity, for he had quite reckoned without the Bailey Sisken Basses who, somewhat exercised by the sudden intrusion of the leather-aproned and -lunged movers in the still hours of the night, burst hotly from the rooms of their butler and maid respectively, causing poor Oggle almost to reconsider the wisdom of his impulsive manoeuver. For, as the old saying would have it, often what is done with rash intent may as surely reap dissent.

But in this event, Oatis Oggle, after suing the Bailey Sisken

Basses for lack of moral torportude, was not only enabled to return with a considerate fortune to his own spouse, but even more easily persuaded to squander the interest alone on a truly fetching young lady who brought him nothing save unremitting happiness and ill-concealed satisfaction.

Alas, Lust, even more than Greed, is what makes racehorses.

PERPETUAL EMOTION OR HOW-COME A GATOR IN THE LOBBY?

A traveling Contortionist & a Clergyist's shy sister'n law were comforced by don't of no rooms be ye dad'n dame a New England type night to spend in such a blizzard never seen in Hell even! In that period every decent hotel strictly observed the ordinance behooving Bundling--it wasn't the cold give them blue noses. Wicked flesh be sure they'd heard of. Hence the serpent-like Beast near the sign-in desk-ask that pair a love! Odd buffer...& him ticklish to boot!

SURE CURE FOR A COLD

In an ugly tan pisgahwva there once lived a Rhodacary. A long low whistle from being ugly, on any hand she looked all made of little birds, which someone had sewed together with very special care.

Now one day a big yellowmustached Frankxgillett, who was every bit as keen as a bucket of frozen gravel, happened to sit down on her in the plumbing fixtures works where she modeled furniture for 'those ladies who demand that ethereal touch,' as the ads proudly phrased it. He later explained that he was under the impression somebody musta left their bearskin on the seat; for, among much else, he was also addicted to footballing.

So, scarcely more than a few weeks had passed when, rather than suffer his snuffling proposals at any greater length, the Rhodacary's mother, herself an accomplished eavesdripper, proceeded to give her talented daughter's consent to the unhappy union. For that is exactly what it turned out to be.

On the very afternoon of the wedding itself the groom, doubtless thinking to show off his great wealth, rammed a thick stack of fifty dollar bills down the throat of the wrong horse. To be sure, not every young bride is fortunate enough to see her new

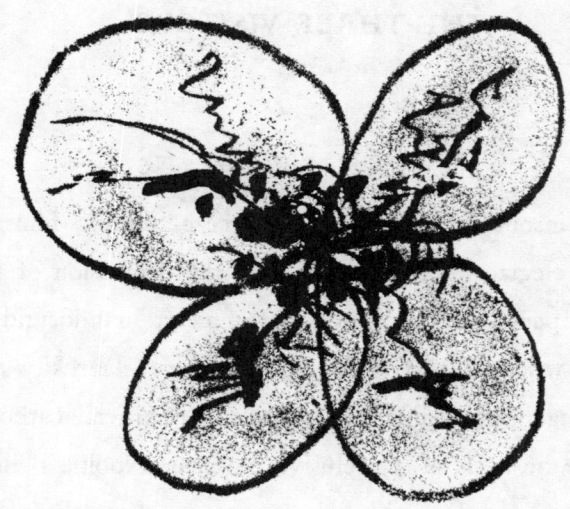

husband buried with a good luck sign planted square in the middle of his forehead. The horse, whose professional name was Loonbait Louie, was ordered stuffed, after first being given one shot for the money.

And our no longer poor but even lovelier Rhodacary, her own mistress at last, went rapidly to pieces— first to one which jutted up out of the top of a great dreary rock called nyny, from whence, amid the shrill cawing of yellow cabs and the gilty sobbing of many another wee wren forced to glow in plush pens lined by whole and leering hawgs, she sent many touching and thoughtful gifts to her dear dear mother. Among them, an almost new pennant with Yarvard on one side and Hale on the other, for, while she wanted to send her mother off on the right cultural foot, so to speak, she also dearly wanted to do all she reasonably could to avoid those stupid factional fights which so often spring up in homes reserved for indigent old ladies.

THE THREE VISITORS

An insouciant little Pelagic Breeze, finding himself in somewhat elegiacal surroundings with the declension of night, stealthway penetrated into the shanty of a certain unjocund Cupfashioner, where, dismayed by the powdery glabrosity of his host, he began, ebulliently, to cozen some exiticial catholicon.

Soft on the heels of a prelusive moment, Nookie Belle, the arcadian mistress of an old codger gone only recently hibernal, tapped ever so tridently on the circus posters which hung in pragmatic abandon under the stained lintel. "Are you there, Mr. Tessis?" softly, softly she called.

"Why, yes, of course, where else?" the dry-cheeked little Pelagic Breeze replied with stridulous haste, emboldened out of all countenance.

"Ah, then, I'm not too late! That is good, good, very good indeed; for, you see, dear Mr. Tessis, I've fetched you a quantity of real clay, clay of the earth, earthy kind... So now, oh now, my dear Mr. Tessis, you won't have to go on hacking bits out of your own flesh, so to speak..."

But our little Pelagic Breeze was already well into his third ocean before the young goddess, who was as beautiful as she was kind, got anywhere near to catching on to the lie.

If perfection could be practiced by everybody, what a very, very mournful noise would assail those soft white ears up there!

MOONDOGG AND THE ONE-ARMED DENTIST'S SISTER

Under silver maskery of hours like frozen waves— when those whom eternity accosts have palely come— within sound of the chimney's gray-petalled wound, Moondogg quietly waits, waits for the maiden of gray tears to climb to a place beside him.

Blurred golden eyes peer up from the winding motorway, while furry lids softer than a bat's nipples open and close over harbor and listening vineyards, silhouettes against which the grieving hands of fogbells vainly beat... peril and longing bedded down like sad crones in a stuff any child might pick apart as easily as that hangman of romance the cottony breath of a thief falsely accused (perhaps of one's very own family)...

Now, in the only moment for that, she climbs, like a struggle

of scissors, to where the sky ends so unimportantly in a roof— the sky which is an animal will ride or rest on almost anything, trains, used grapeskins, heads of sick old whores, slopping up and down in crummy roominghouses ready, at the droop of a rat, to go off on the gaffing route if they so much as get an uncancelled postcard from some daughter or other who thinks she's too good to watch a hairy blue duck making a batch of fudge unless she has her pink, formal gloves on—; thereupon Moondogg inquired, "Well— that is, tell me first, did you have a nice day?" and he falls to kissing her dangling arms and forehead.

Birds of ice with blunted gray beaks tear at the shrouding waves. O then sobbing into his cruel pale curls, she will answer: "Take me with you! O now take me, take me with you... In three weeks less a day I shall be fiftyseven years old.

"O the songs and tales you have given me of your world. — Soon, soon whatever might have been for me... look! the cold long dark, and I have had no life I have never lived at all..." She continued on in this vein for some little while.

Moondogg let her chatter herself quite out, then, grinning he uncoiled one protracted statement after the other, each seeming to have more flurry about nothing than the other...

"... and so my father made an absolute, a preposterously final sort of fool of himself; I know I, for one, excusing the expression, would never have thought it feasible to have, say, well—, *pink* lilies growing up out of horsemanure— would you? truly now, would you? Of course not! It's positively vulgar, if not disgusting... Scarce wonder they locked him out."

"Take me away! O take me away with you!"

Hungrily in and out run his white tongues, and Moondogg says with kindness strange (and roll waves of pitiless wonder! the faces shaped in ice and the fire born of the watching darkness): "Cling you fast in upon my belly. Hold there. Hold— In the color of tears is the speech of mankind made; in that of skulls the bravest squeak from any bright old lad... Watch it now! I may prove a bit... ticklish."

"Oh, there's one other thing," she pants up through his stiff, cold fur. "Please fly me through that damn brother of mine's office just once more before we set off. Oh boy... Oh boy...! (I left the windows all open.) Oh, boy! Wait'll that prissy bum gets a load of *us!*"

Fortunately there still are ways of teaching dentists not to shove their arms halfway down the throats of nervous patients.

GAUNT EVE IN THE MORNIN'

It was one of those days that seem to make their way in without anybody noticing much about it. Mrs. Arglutt folded her sweaters and waited.

Pretty soon Juggie the Boddy-Fann arched his short though lithe body over the curb. Oh, yes, Mrs. Arglutt thought. There's you all right— and next it'll be that sleazy gilled postman! Oh, yes, and him all as shy as a beat-up lark on last summer's hammock. And suddenly her musing took an audible direction: "I wonder. Oh, yes, I do at that. I just got me a hunch that it do a bit of whistlin', too. *Him— him* and those pretentious sleeve bands and gold bead moccasins of his!"

And there he was. It was exactly ten of eight, not one iota different from any other day! There he was peering in through the window on the sunporch, his glinty ox's eyes fixed on her person. — "I just know I must look like a big pink sponge... Oh, what a habit to get into!" Mrs. Arglutt said, pretending to address a stack of those old fashioned postcards which specialize in winter scenes and reary skirted bathers on long closed beaches. One after the other she lifted her woolen, salmon colored sweaters from their adjoining stack and pressed them over her swirling chest. Behind her a pane in the reinforced window tinkled out— Oh, damn! Mrs. Arglutt thought, her blush deepening perceptibly, whether from exasperation or the sudden snuffling at her shoulder blades, it would be hard to say. "That's the fourth this week already," she mumbled with a little shiver of nervous excitement.

And then at last the clock was clanging the hour. — *Now* she could breathe again, he was gone. Like that-poof!

When she felt her strength returned enough she sighed into her corset, meanwhile waddling first forward then back in the imitation hip dance she'd picked up at one of her perennial Saturday movies— and it was not until she had shrugged her slip and torn kimono-style housecoat down over her frizzy, graying hair that she permitted herself a half-petulant, half-gleeful speculation: Oh, yes, oh yes indeed! First it was that great silly, mustard-flecked mustache of yours, then it was those two geranium-pot-red shredded wheats you stuck on yourself for eyebrows— Oh, yes, you sure handed me a laugh with those correspondence school disguises of yours, dearie! And, next— Ah, but why should I look ahead to spoil your fun! You poor silly... who could miss knowing that big foot-long nose of yours? Let alone all bandaged out like a basket of diapers.

And suddenly Mrs. Arglutt sank down on an old sofa whose torn cover was littered with movie and confession magazines—and lowering her swollen gray face into her fat, braceletted arms, she began, helplessly, to cry. And Mrs. Arglutt thought: Ah, yes, there'll come the mornin' when you swallow that precious government whistle of yours altogether... And oh then it'll be that I have to watch the split ends of its string disappearing like the sad whiskers of some modern snake down to investigate the congestion of still another poor apple.

THE UNCLAIMED BEAVER

One foul day an Inamcshoon was squatting beside a wishbone vine thinking 'Better a rich young man's playtoy than something a poor old duffer would come round all the time dropping his cheap gray cigar ashes and hair on,' when a big Chuckbailey, its gold tooth slicked back from receding lips, presented and gave voice: "With you over there, Honay, and me cossing away yonder here, no wonder our youngins have had to wait so long for their own proper and fittin' parents..."

Then the Inamcshoon cried in a doubt: "Oh sweet bits! If only that candle of yours had a light on it, a bad half the women in town would be well singed."

High above them, in a shiny bald cypress, a twain of little scarlet bushtits were acrobirding happily, their gray chests and greener feet contrasting in brilliance with the heavy, dullish fragrance of the needles and the darkness, which had just pitched down. Like a bear begging the arm of some reluctant hunter, the Chuckbailey fetched its hand out and called again: "Then they finally did get round to planting your old man, huh?"

"Well, y-es, that was all right, after he had turned down every drink of good corn we kep' a-offerin' him— hell, it went on like that for purty nears better'n two weeks. He was always stubborn, Pa was, but not *that* stubborn. But now you take the old 'oman— all us kids got to callin' her that from Pa, I reckon — now *she'd* shove you real close on some dang pipped-up thinkin', she would. Well, now, sir, when she went 'long to the buryin'. — Stop your doin' thet! Oh that poor old 'oman, jest like a bitty little bald baby, 'septin' she had kinda spotted gray hair that grows right down past her chest— There we was, as I said, all a-standin 'blowin' our nose and things, when Jed he looks round. 'Now where'd thet old 'oman go!' Jed he says, —all jumpy like.

"Poor little ragged greasy thing... You know how curious she allus used to be aboutin' holes—"

"S'ppose you mean that old 'oman Ma of yours?" put in the big Chuckbailey.

"'Member that old long fur hat she'd wear most like a piece of cardboard you'd plaster up a window with— Why, hell, she even wore it on her head to the attic. That's where she did her sleepin'."

"This is that old 'oman Ma of yours, you're a-fixin' to tell me about?"

"Wull naow—" went on the yaller haired Inamcshoon. "Thet

old long fur hat hain't on hits nail 'bove the woodshed dooar. And I *jest know* she'd be a-comin' lookin' for it onless... onless'n somethin' was a-holdin' her down— Like, say, mebby a little ole hole in the groun'..."

"Thet's a mighty good way of doin' things. I once't had an old grandpap allus uster 'clare: 'Boay, Ah figgers hit a-this'n way— Dirt is jist erbout the oney meat nobody kin complain of not gittin' enough of.' So-o— Let's you and me fry us up a little chicken, huh?"

HE DIDN'T KNOW THE SON WAS LOADED

An Edodell, one quite late and starless night, believing that the window belonged to a certain Maziefeccio, climbed instead into the one of a Mrspjjones, with the resulting dislodgement of several pots, among them one for flowers and two for a somewhat more fugitive usage.

"Whatever are they yelling about down there, Herbert?" a sleepy voice greeted him from the darkness.

"Beg pudon, I think you've made a mistake, too," the Edodell simply replied. He was under average tall, salloweyed, given to stealing furtive glances at the legs of horses on circus posters.

"Eeh— So I have. Oh, *here's* the lightcord. Damn, for a minute there I thought somebody was pulling at the pigtail of my wig. But, you see, I have made a mistake. Just between us, *my* Herbert would never dream of going to call on a strange lady with a wet pantsfront showing. Besides—" and she chuckled, revealing a set of uneven gums— "the funny thing is, Herbert has been dead for well on to twenty-three years now. He was what they used to call a trainchaser. Poor dear. You see, he finally *did* catch one, a great big shiny rootsnorter of a one, but wouldn't you just know, the damned thing was going the wrong way. But here I am jawin' away while I'll bet you're hungry enough to eat a mess of Arizona sardines without even botherin' to open the can. You'll find some in the drawer of the bureau that big galvanized pot I used to keep geraniums in rolled under."

At a lack of anything more exciting to do, the Edodell spent two long thumbnails accepting her kind invitation, dripping self-consciously from one foot to the other as he did so. When hi! lo! out of the bureau drawer sprang a little guy who, brandishing an old-fashioned horsepistol, cried: "No ornery galoot is agonta hold up this here stage coach while old Houston Herbie Junior's on deck!"

Then, after an abrupt, soiled herringbone twinkling, the Mrspjjones said proudly, "That was sure a smart move changin' them house numbers. Reckon that must be about the twelfth-thirteenth tonight already."

"Shull's I close what's left of the winder now, Maw?"

"Shore you kin, Son. The sooner you git that new one up, and the pots all back in their place, the better it'll be. But fust, throw his pants down onto the runnin' board of that crockery cart he fell into— Mmm... two sawbucks and a trey of fins in his hippocket. This rate, we soon kin go off a-lookin' round for your Paw down the shaft of thet goldmine somewheres in good ole Nevady City. Twenty-odd years is a long time, Son, — and with thet good sharp haid of your Paw's, who knows what he may've struck by now."

TAT FOR TWO

When Harry and Edgar were little boys in very gay ratatan shortsuits their mothers were in habit of taking them, either on tedious hikes, that were oftentimes depressing and tiring as well, or to see the former's Aunt Nettie, a formidable and notoriously predatory woman.

However, this frequently turned out rather better than any of them had any real right to expect, for not only are things someways offpoint in sober prospect, they are even more occasionally no less keenly absurd from the vantage furnished by memory. Certainly even the most quiescently supercilious of individuals would have been forced, and that, readily, to the admission of some considerable hesitation in regard to the moral advisability of taking such mere pips of circumstance to visit "*that* woman."

In the very first place, to begin only there, there was the temptation— and what a very real one it was!— instinct in an unshaved leg... More might be said— much, much more... However—!

Is it worth saying that little Harry and Edgar lost a moment in succumbing to an opportunity of such attraction (and menace) to their as yet nascent talents? We think it is, and for a reason no more complex or convoluted than this: Our little sillies, despite all the bravery of their tanned salmon colored, wedge shaped caps and equally aggressive nonchalance, had promptly and joyously leapt upon that very particular moment as being the most convenient envelope for the enclosure of a bit of sprightly goldfish-strawing— the one useable momento of their increasingly irksome hiking expeditions.

Oh well may you ask: What is worse than a bad woman? And oh well may we answer: Why, man— What else but a good one cut in two...

BOTTOMS UP

Now once there was a Roydabbit who, to offset a strong tendency to the puny, had at last weakly given way to the temptation of fancying himself a weightlifter, now (fortunately) unemployed.

He lived in a small hollow nokomisill with a ribcovered Berthamae and an old hairbrimmed grumpus named Maknowsbest, both of whom claimed to have his number, the one that comes just before one.

It chanced that one very buickiful morning, as dark sandhued vines of claustrodioxide were weaving round the huge happy green poster which acted as steeple on the almytbuckian chapel, the Roydabbit was just in point of emerging from a drugstore with a set of fencing foils, two boxes of greenish banana shaped generators and half a dozen coils of highly magnetized wire, when he happened to fall in with his loudly gesticulating mate and female parent. The former, luckily, was protected by hipboots and a rubber bee hunter's mask and cape. But Maknowsbest— ah, she proved herself to be a tale with a somewhat different end.

It had befallen that some years before she had been hit in

the head by a wedge while out stretching her legs on a motor trip one day through the north woods. However, with little more than the loss of a clump of rather badly worn hair, some visiting firemen did succeed in breaking her sudden and irresistible attraction for the exercising wire. Indeed, they brought her to with such extremely diligent care that Maknowsbest spent the next few days leading them in window busting forays on all the neighboring towns around, and wasn't ever quite sober again until she passed on through a window in a signboard eight stories above the scatteringly crowded main street.

But poor Roydabbit— ah, he was surrounded immediately by a glad crying group of Katinkajoneses, their distinctive markings clearly revealed under their coats of volley ball and beach umbrellaing: "Oh do show us that handpress again!" "*And* those fascinating pushups!" "When does our turn come to stand on your shoulders?" And so saying each grasped a foil and was sent shooting upward to the magnetized wire. —

"Oh!" "Oh!" "Oh!" "Oh!" — And oh how the Roydabbit's thin knees did bulge down over his shoetops, just with the strain of holding that spinning catherine wheel up out of reach of a throng of salesmen in a definite buying mood.

And oh how they spun and spun and spun... those swirling

fleshpink lilies — "Oh!" "Oh!" "Oh!" "Oh!" — A dazzling raiment indeed... while like a rain of petals down from the jackknifing necks of so many swans, a scatter of middy blouses and gay black silk shorts and badminton sandals... falling, falling on the bemussed crowd... And yet, oddly enough, the voice of the Berthamae contained an unmistakable note of severity in it as she declared: "So! You bent-leg bum you— Now I know why you come home at all hours with footprints smeared all over your nice clean shirts!"

And with a vestige of grim hauteur she broke one of the banana shaped generators from its box, — She sighted carefully up at the pinkly twirling petals. — And she let fly. —

"Oh!" "Oh!" "Oh!" "Oh!" — "Ooooh!"

CHICKEN FRIED IN HONEY

Clarence Snull, who had come to suspect that heaven needed more than one penny candle for proper lighting, found himself by easy degrees with the yearn to marry nicely and to live, if not happily, then at least with all his appetites, be they corporal or even of a less spiritual sort, something more than just well taken care of. For his part, let it be said now, he wanted something other than people customarily put in their hair; so far was this true, that it was the local Croesus, a Teddia Henatoe, who had unconsciously managed to insinuate herself in his.

Now the late Baron Wartley had been a noisy, foulmouthed oaf, with considerably more than an ordinary penchantius as a cut-up; and perhaps never more so than on the occasion of his being clawed to death by a nesting ibis which he had locked away in the cellar with one of his poorer nephews. Although this happened a good twenty years ago, that small boy is not only still bald but the most careful and extreme caution must be exercised in choosing maids of a peculiar type whose only duty is to sit very quietly on his head at night.

But however haunted in life she was by her husband's grammatical nastities, even Teddia will be the first to admit that the

Baron does lay most goldenly indeed now. You will remember that it was he who patented The Spokey Hula Queen, a phonebooth not to be confused with the Inquisition's much gentler "Iron Maiden"; and to his credit, too, must go that innocent-appearing seat cushion which has proved so useful in throwing strangers together at church socials — we refer, of course, to the famous Wartley Simulated-Elephant Windbreaker.

So one spring morning Clarence went bouncing off in hopes of receiving a good account for himself. "I just only hope she's not down in the garden pavilion with Torgas as usual," he told himself with the tone of one snuffling dead cigar ash through a borrowed straw. Now and then a small boy passed whistling shrilly, a long grimacing line of cows trailing behind him, tails held stiffly aloft under a brilliant gaiety of balloons. On the edge of a brown field and a barnroof an old woman with an eggcrate clutched under either arm was staring reproachfully up at a rusted tin weathercock, whose days of usefulness even in his special province were long since down the drain. From time to time she smote the tobacco colored gingham at her knee and spat disgustedly into the creaking wind.

Noticing on a sudden a fence of barbed rails Snull thoughtfully slapped his election buttoned beret upon first one raised sneaker then the other and declared: "I bet Torgas only rented that flashy admiral's suit of his. Besides, I'll fire the rat!— I mean, besides, I don't consider him to be a very good butler, anyway." With which happy decision behind him, he was able, after several false starts, to succeed almost in clearing by the crotchfirst method the dungaree-pennanted fence. A painfully short while after this experience he encountered the widow of his dreams emerging from a bamboo pavilion, the butler Torgas close as a mustard plaster at her elbow. From head to foot both were dressed entirely in feathers.

"Well, well. . ." Clarence declared, in a masterful effort to show himself equal to any emergency.

"Chicken pickin'," the butler Torgas remarked with a nonchalance that nearly smacked of the laconic, as he began rapidly to fashion a row of impromtu epaulettes across his downy, wirehaired chest.

"Oh Mr. Snull!" cried Teddia Wartley-Henatoe all in a flustery splutter. "It seems that Gassie and I have just had the most darling experience, but not only that, my dear Mr. Snull— Oh could you ever guess, I wonder! we've had an even more darling omen, as well! Do you remember— but of course you don't! But, *anyhow,* there used to be all along the ceiling a whole shelf of enormous crocks simply cram full of honey. Well!" And laughing happily she threw herself under Torgas the butler's protective wing— "They're not there now, Mr. Snully-Wully... *And* we're planning to fly right off and get married!"

After they had gone, Clarence walked glumly into the pavilion and throwing himself on the torn-up mattress, burst into laughter and tears; for his sweat shirt was ripped in several places.

HOW OSTRICHES CAME TO HAVE THROATS LONG ENOUGH TO GET GOLF BALLS STUCK IN THE MIDDLE OF

Her tail tied in a slipknot to a pink ogeechee lime tree by a mischievous young Ostrich, the Fearsame Queen of the Jungle regarded dourly the thrashed, flat tundra, brooding perhaps of some hard way of returning the compliment. So, most sweetly at last she called: "Oh Audry, honey chile, I am so ferociously pleased that you have honored me with your ingenious prank." Whereupon brightly the little Ostrich shuffled gulpingly forward off the links, his demeanor an open scorn of the whole race of caddies, who, it would certainly seem spend most of their time dashing madly about with the seats gone out of their pants. "How come, Queenie kid?" he bawled in a most jerky and disconcerting fashion. "Just put your head in here, dearie," the other roared gently, with a drooling nod at his footwork. "And when I pull, you back up and see if you can kick that stupid boy with the nettle briars stuck all over his rear elbow."

Better to be threatened with a bad rule than measured with a good rope.

A CASE OF UNMISTAKABLE IDENTITY

The Great Detective was called to a small, worried town to investigate a report of blue people. "To begin with," he told the constable in charge, who was vainly trying to unlock his handcuffed wrists with a buttonhook borrowed from an old hip-yellow-shoed temperance worker whom many a drunk had taken a shine to, "I smell that you've been drinking. And at a horse trough— that much I don't need my long, bent microspipe for: unless, bore this in mind, that's just your own personal way of trying to disguise yourself as a skunk of loose habits."

Glancing idly through the cobwebs which served for windows, he watched two lovers carrying eager, naked blankets thread their way through the crowd, which consisted of a small man in a lavender beret who was stealing occasional glances at an undeveloped roll of film. Then, noticing that several savage cows were about to catch the eight o'clock train just short of the station, he thought quite enough time had been wasted on this particular case, and proceeded to solve it without further delay: "I happened to notice," he said, "a nudist colony just as the train almost tips over from a sudden weight-shift up along the cliff there. And I know, too, that you boys have been doing an uncommon

amount of fingerprint-taking lately— So, quite naturally, since there is no way of knowing where their sleevecuffs end, you've just been forced to do what I'd call a good, all-over job of it."

Hence it is that man is the only oyster with a head of hair that people are always putting and taking woolen drawers on and off of.

NOT ALL TOWELS COME FROM TURKEY

Innate modesty and poverty are, at best, little governable under even the most propitious circumstances; but, with a doting mother round his neck, and the sympathy of his elders scarcely more than a vague, withdrawn belching over feasts rather less palpable than unseen, Gus B. Marblecake finally applied for and was got to the position of head dryer in Mrs. Suddsineri's, an establishment where women only old might tea and soak in the past and far hotter steam.

There, soapfooting about from one grayly streaming stool to the next (in need of a touch of mansage): or: (perhaps just for a friendly jab up under the badly torn robe that had to be bought fresh each morning), poor Gus had his work clucked out for him keeping 'the balls a-bearing' — a phrase much favored by Ma Goatbane, whose idea of hirsute decorum demanded a sight more from him than the customary mustache-trimming.

But what irritated him to the point of diving suddenly over benches into open lye vats, when all the doors of the reducing cabinets happened to be rudely closed to him, was to have his mother grate round like an old disheveled possum pup, her long toenails squirking into his adams apple while she'd say something perhaps like: "Whyinel don't you go out and come back with a nice big bottle of ice cold beer? Or at least a shave! You couldn't have been listening very good!— I'm your mother, and pretty damned tired acting like a little bare two-faced Moses up in these here bushes!"

An ass loaded down with the burden of another is never more doubly so.

EVEN THE KRAKEN MUST HAVE HIS SPIEL

There was once a gently made Kraken under whose frontal neck squirmed a row of spindling green legs which culminated in badly worn carpet slippers, and these, in the main, of dubious fit. Now this did not for long escape the envious notice of his grumpy comrades; so, after a few short centuries, they gave him pain to realize that his continued presence was regarded as being not only strictly undesirable to them but positively anathematical to every cherished ideal of krakendom.

So — go he must; and that, unslowly. The night was cold ... even colder on land; close above tenebrous star huddles twitched grimly. Our poor, bewildered friend came ... at dripping last... to a house, a very big one, impressive with two front doors, and even supplied with an auxiliary cellar just under the driveway. Here, thank god!! lights were lit! and on a high balcony a thousand Persian horns were being softly agitated. At any rate, it was s-o-m-e-t-h-i-n-g!

Propelling his ice-corroded muzzles against a sweeping fret of windowpanes, to his glad delight he was instantly overjoyed to behold a wonderfully splendid table before which lolled a good five and seventy wee sapid orphans, a profusion of crumbs and buttons fatly popping off their greasy-snug suits.

Is it any wonder that, with some impatience, he beckoned to a lovely suede-faced lady in a low-cut shawl of peeling gold mesh whose legs were bowed nearly as double as her chin under frosty trays of sugar cookies and champagne buckets? but ah, how slowly, even so, did she roll to the massive, harpists'-picks-studded gate... *there!* at last she is throwing back the first bolt, and now another, another another, until all twenty three have been thrown! — "Good-evening, Mrs. Herbcrest," she greeted him warmly. "I scarcely recognized you without the glasses you borrowed from me early last summer. Land's sake, I do hope you haven't broken them... I've been eating any number of silly things, bits of teacups, part of that greedy little Thompson girl's finger... why, only day before yesterday I toasted up a whole set of my very prettiest napkins. How amused the children were to see me drinking yellow coffee, dear, dear things... I'm a dunker, you know."

"Never mind that," interjetted the impatient Kraken. "Those pleasant little minnows there—" indicating the orphans, who were now contentedly belting one another with the planks their steaks had come on, "I know damn well that their shoes will fit me. Only thing is, I wouldn't want to hurt their feelings... so I guess I'll have to eat them first."

"Oh, I understand perfectly, perfectly, Mrs. Herbcrest," the lady said soothingly. "Just let me set this tray down somewhere, and I'll pitch right in and help you. For after all, Agatha, you *are* the president of our little welfare club."

To your true bird-watcher few events can arouse quite the same excited comment as the spectacle of a newly hatched brood of cowey-grackles floating serenely on a set of rusty old bedsprings.

HOW PEPPER CAME TO BE DISCOVERED

The door which separated the three rooms opened and a boy carrying a large bronze vessel and a scales such as cowl-weavers use entered. He looked tired and about him. The leafy curtains flapped through the boarded up windows in the direction of the orchard. Someone had made an effort to cover a series of gaping holes in the wall by plastering strips of folded newspapers over them, but now these were yellowed and revealed minute scratches across more than one bathing beauty. While through the shattered panel of the door, a heavy, shiny-badged face could be dimly seen, as well as the tip of an ink-stained ear. A fire of sticks in a copper wicket swung from the charred rafters, in this fashion providing the only illumination. In the castle up the flag-decked river, where lived a certain lonely Queen, the above description would go a-beggaring, indeed. Toward evening, having chewed, since earliest morning, an incessant amount of very salty fish pieces, she decided to go out for a drink, one of the faucets being clogged with the undependable nose of the royal plumber.

But unfortunately in her haste she did not at once remember the river nor notice that the utensil which the senile old king had

tossed down to her from one triple-chinned, frizzy-whiskered tower window was made carelessly of straw, for it was little more than a pot-of-emergency. So after having fallen in and quite spoiled her regal gown, if not her moon-enhanced appearance, dip and redip as she might, only a dank taste like from spoiled feathers rewarded her. It was then that the head of a poor crabfisher breasted the water a little to the fore of her side, and mistaking her for one of common clay, led her at golden, blushing length to the star-tiaraed bank. It was not until many, many years later that someone happened to stumble upon the old king at the foot of a deep well, grinning broadly down upon a tin drinking cup which he had been unable to uncollapse. And at least in one humble shack in a distant and pleasant spot just around a heavily-thicketted bend in the river, there is someone whose fish are seasoned with something a bit snappier than salt.

Better to be the carelessly handled bauble of a spiny young drip, than the unused rack of some pointless old umbrella.

THE EVOLUTION OF THE HIPPOPOTAMUS

Once a horse, a gawky countryboy, a striptease queen and an old featherduster decided to set up house together in a sort of windmill which had been newly remodeled to their purpose and specifications.

Everything went along very smoothly indeed until one cold, foggy morning Orker S. Wilkins, the horse, took it into his thick head to try out for the local swimming team. — "All for the glit o' a few cheap and sordid medals," as Fu-Fu Rita chose to express the general sentiment.

So nothing, of course, would do but they must all leave off where they were and go trudging up Old Sorghum Holler to the 'Grocknest Invitational', with R. C. Dasey, the countryboy, a-clutching a rusty hayfork in one hand and Granny Turkis in the other.

Oh, it was cruel! most cruel! How those rural people chortled and guffawed when poor Wilkins, that swollen with a false and silly pride as to have quite forgotten to cut a tail-hole in his suit, proceeded to plunge out into the very middle of the river— only to ignominiously drown!

Returned to the garish merry-go-round, the three survivors

sadly gawked or shapely-strippered or fluttered rather dankly, each after his or her individual fashion. Before long, however, Granny Turkis, gnawing slyly on the handle of her wire-feathered duster, remarked: "He-he-he— Heh... Oh that golldinged silly boy Wilkins! He just never did have no fair chance to outgrow that ticklish tendency of his, no-how... Go easy on the aqua with my next one, R. C. Hell, that's the least we kin do for him now..."

Even a sieve is water-tight at the bottom of a deep well.

THE HOTEL BLUES

Maimie, Jillanne, Pretty Thing, Doris Ebikuzhlavshy and the Nanary Bell have come on a routine visit. They are arguing much too noisily, and smoking long, black, lace-fringed cigarettes. One of the Sklegg boys (perhaps Tim or Little Nob) is with them, but since he is just along to look down the fronts of their blouses, he is content to say nothing. Even though, in that same lobby, stands a penniless clerk named Lemuel Clayfoot who has had the uncommon bad luck to fall in love with a rich old garment known fat and wide as Mrs. Thistledown.

To be sure, they are now in the midst of trying to figure out what to do with Lem's svelte-structured young wife, for most happily old Thissie is already safely locked up in a wall vault in his own private den. "I suppose we could tell her that we are only going off together to hunt leopards with elephants," suggested the loot-smitten clerk the next morning. (As it happened, he had just discovered a secret panel some hundred and eighty soft brown feet to the left of the vault.)

"That would hardly be fair," sighed Mrs. Thistledown, as she scraped her heavily rouged, piebald nag out from under a low-hanging branch, and rode baldly on ahead. "For the elephant is a bit bigger, don't you know."

Lem, rising abruptly to the occasion of finding still another set of her teeth on his saddle, besides the one which had lodged itself down his neck when they had stopped last near an old hollow log to change her splintered leg, declared, "I do get the impression, what with your obvious belief in full preparedness, that we should have a very peaceful time of it together." And spurring his steed stealthily back to the mansion, Clayfoot sped down to the gameroom and wrenched the panel open all in one gulp, greeting each of the ninety dancing girls warmly by name as she floated like an unusually clear September Morn forth into his arms.

Fear the united from the front, the democracy from the arsenal, and the general bringing up any rear save his own.

HOW THE SLINGSHOT CAME TO BE INVENTED

A Leopard, whose glasses had been fitted in a most helter-high-water fashion, went out one gray day a-deering, and in his short-sighted haste chanced to make prey of a Missionary's Spouse. Whereupon the latter said:

"Oh Huldred dear, I wonder if you would very much mind leaving your work long enough to come and save me...?"

Great sibilant leaves that were tanned a deep, brooding turtle color by long exposure to 'old-him-mucha-blig-bright-fellah-dam-dam-maybeso-allasame-me-pore-hurryhup-heathem-blast-ard' (the colorful native way of saying sun), stirred like a flutter of kneecaps on the knobby limbs of the boombah palms which could be dimly discerned through the smokehole of an empty hut near the outskirts of the village. Here, stretched to bursting upon a hammock made of discarded inner tubes, sleeps the kindly old Chief Rango Buum in an orange tuxedo with white lapels and leg stripes, which is at least more than several sizes too small for him; while a couple small brown feet away creeps ever nearer and nearer a penknife held laughingly in the little fist of one of his four hundred-odd sons, the even ones having all long since been declared illegitimate and sold off to a pet shop whose

speciality is catering to the better class of angel. Some distance removed the sky has the unmistakeable air of someone lying on a rush mat with a lovely, sixteen year old maiden, against whose shimmering, tight fitting skin great blossoms of flashing teeth-of-paradise look very shabby indeed.

After what might be considered a seemly interval the Missionary inquired, not unkindly: "Uh-err... Did I hear you say something just then, Agnes?"

"Why, yes, I hope you did, Reverend," answered his wife, her words punctuated by a series of mounting growls. "It was my thought that you might see your way to dropping your work for a moment, and so find yourself in a better position to come into the jungle a bit for the purpose of saving me; ouch—"

Then running pensive fingers through the fragrant leaves of dark blossoms, and with a somewhat impatient glance over a soft and very pretty shoulder, Huldred the Missionary said, "But really now, Agnes. I must say— it hardly impresses me as being fitting and proper that I should have made an arduous, self-annulling journey half again around this sinful earth for the rather commonplace mission of saving *you*, my dear."

But, as it happened, his solicitude, by reason of a succession of fortuitous events, went almost unnoticed. For perhaps the most circumstantial of these, in the unfettered person of good Chief Rango Buum, descended without further ado on the galvanized back of Bertie Enner Gene the ^{00}th, whose teeth we have forgotten to say had been fitted by that same nervous optometrist. And with a violent nod at the Missionary's helpmeat, whom another of his odd little sons was helping up with a homemade bugle-bagpipe combination, the kindly old Chief went hastily riding off through a huge bolo-bongo tree. On which happy note we, too, must take our leave of the great and mysterious jungle's vociferously colorful and rapidly clearing.

MOONSHINE AND HAWGJOWL

On a stool in the Lady of the Black Lilies Lunchroom, having a cuppa easy on the canned cowjuice cawffee, Buck Reluquerro glanced at the classy little blonde gentereen who was unselfconsciously rubbing an overflow of lipstick off on the front of his lemon-pink shirt.

While outside...

A strung-out cluster of pigeons peeling in the moldy gray sun — or are they houses? and fluttering bunches of molting grapes ... clacking their thin beaks over scaling backfences— or are they perhaps a gossip of a slightly rarer feather, with their markings of interminable brooms and mops and buckets and tales? And across the street three men leisurely flying from a hardware, heaped-up screens on their little bawling boy-drawn cart.

Sometimes the world almost seems too big damn fine and sassy...

Dressed stylishly in a cut-away frock of a brilliant, faded boatred, like the underside of a rubber parrot swathed in wilting rose petals, an old lady mowing figure eights in Mayor Stallfetter's lawn. While in the arbor behind the new shoemaker's, a scene of mounting slacktivity, — much as you might expect to find in a place that had just been left by eleven half-asleep giantesses, each more eager than the last to leave nothing worldover behind...

So Buck Reluquerro introduced himself to his pleasant little stool-mate and said:

"Yeah, same here. Thought I hadn't seen you around town before. Well, anyway, this time I'm telling you about, my old man was out back watering up the pigs when I drove in with Erebella. She was my day-old bride, see. At eighty Pa still makes a lotta folks chuckle when they first meet him. That's because since my Maw died he's taken up the idea that he's one of them old fashioned iron bathtubs where come a Saturday night the whole family kin wash all at once. Course they's always someone round to encourage a person like that, only in his case it's the whole blame hebang of Sauley brothers. They humor him along-like — eatin' the grub right outten his old saggy mouth, sleepin' seventeen abreast in his old sassy bunk, and twiceth the week plumb half drownin' the old boy into the bargain.

"An', like I'm tellin' you, just as I git Erebella dragged up to them, where they be round the pigs, Pa is a-sayin', 'See thet? I told you fellers my overflow valve was a-gittin' clogged.' An' one of them Sauley brothers he says, 'Shall's I let this little red-eyed hawg up thin?'

"Then I says, 'Pa', I says, 'I want fur you to meet my new one-day-old wife. Pa Reluquerro, I want's you should meet the new Mrs. Reluquerro.'

"So without turnin' round at all, Pa he says, 'Buck, you git me thet big wrench from the bucket on the mantel beside yer Uncle Pludgurkle's photey. En if she's not thear, try under them wet towels we got on top of your Maw down in the cellarway."

"So I says, 'Noaw don't you be gittin' too onreckonable, Pa,' I says. 'I've brung Erebella all the ways from Kalamazoo just on purpose she should meet you.'

"'*Whall!*' Pa he says real loud like, an' he cradles his arms and his legs up-like to show just how pleased he is. 'Buck, yer're a right smart boy! A chip offen the old tub, even iffin I do say so!' An', I'm a sonofa old saggy gray owl with busted suspenders if Pa don't smile right up at my Erebella. An' Pa he says, 'Yessir! Yer a-lookin' at a expert, Ma'am, iffen I do say so m'self. They's oney one model better than what them Kalamazooers be— an' thet's a double bottomed Flint Imperial! Whall! m' purty little ladykins, yer a-lookin' at a good old double bottomed Flint Imperial *right this guddumed minute!*'

"So just then Wilber Sauley— he was standin' three brothers in an' chawin' baccky all up and down ole Snouty Ike's neck (he's the shy one, I think I told you)— So Wilbur he says, 'Would ye like a bit of fresh-yestidey cutplug, Ma'am, Erebellford, please Ma'am?' But— Pa he went right on a-talkin' to my little store-boughten-like bride, an' Pa he says, 'Right after supper, remind me to take a look over your outlet screen. . .'

"I told you easy on that cow, Mac. So's like I was sayin', my Erebella she goes a-tearin' back to the car, darn near a-takin' half of my arm with her, an' she jumps in thet hard the motor and both front wheels come a-flyin' off, an' she kicks out the floorboards with them little purple dancin' shoes of hers— Yeah, with the mustard this time. An' fust thing we know there she is hightailin' it down that old saggy road a-blowin' one of them big purty four notes an' a blue rooster's tail horns thet I jest paid me out my last twenty-nine dollars on for all she's worth!"

Haste, if we are to believe all we hear, is the proof that always seems to go a-chasin' off to spoil somebody else's pudding for us.

THE NUMBER THAT COMES AFTER FEVE

Just about everybody went on the picnic. (And while some were off in the fields falling prone upon gay prone*, others contented themselves with the felling of one swoop**). It might be said that what had been so often told before over the cupboard pillows, was finding new excitements in the retelling. Some $ 300, 007, 000 and 52 c worth of scenery went almost unnoticed in that sizzling Friday afternoon friskforall.

And presently, when the village was having its pre-dark highbell, and larks were beginning to light each pretty house, in that gloaming where every song was a better kind of lamp for what no bed however trundled could do alone, couple after couple— hmmm... The woods were beginning to fill with merry shadows— All there along the flower skirted river, while safely in their stalls vast sullen cows stirring mournfully. Voices were beginning slowly to make themselves heard, as someone... approached... down... the purple tumbling of the hill. "You

---

*) A species of little rose-chested quail, which are often mistaken in maturity for grouse.

**) An oat seldom given to domesticity— although it is occasionally to be found growing under portable Indian blankets and on the saddles of horses born, for the most part, in the last century.

name it, Susan, I'll buy a star down for you any old day." And "Come on, you big kneewet! You're just tetched in the heel, scared of every little thing— just like that bussy-jimpin' ma of yours." and "And there was Uncle Pilgus a-comin' down the lane all cake-eared from his pore ole daddy's wedding." and "So's I just staked it on the ram and come on over to look up my little whomwithal." and, far-off, the taunting of little Bilford Blister: "Mary Ellen's got a stuck on Taffi Johnson... Mary Ellen's got..."

Softly, softly, *fugit hora* with their pleasant *entremets*.

And so we to our story...

That's it.

THE PROFESSIONAL SON

A Candle-Sniffer was returning happily from a miss adventure when he had the fortune to encounter two well balanced cyclists propelling an old lady before them on the gleaming handlebars of their bikes. "If you don't mind me putting my cent in," he said through taut nostrils, "it strikes me you fellows could come up with something rather more interesting to do at this hour." And, with a rapid flick of his forked tongue over his waxy mustache, he smiled a gay reminiscence.

To which counsel the disheveled but happily rapt passenger made instant rejoinder, "Conceivably you are unaware that only as recently as twenty minutes ago our roles presented a somewhat identically contrary appearance. But, even if I was sure you understood that, my fine flame topped boy, what possible point could be made by reminding you— and I must insist on laying considerable stress on this— Where was I? oh yes: *ouch!* What point, indeed? Nevertheless I really feel that I should make it very clear to you that nearly all of the present merriment of these two, er, ah, gentlemen, stems from a circumstance which is no longer tenable, to say the very most."

And with that the little party disappeared around a wall.

The Candle-Sniffer waited until the last floating remnants of the warm seats had dissolved under the cold, dawn breath of a truckload of disgruntled pigs, then thoughtfully he observed, "Who'd ever have figured such a very dried-up old party would have gams long enough to pedal one of them old fashioned style high wheel jobs all by herself— let alone balance a couple fat, bad breathed grizzle bears on her forebars."

"But what I don't get," said a policeman, who had caught a hurried glimpse of the scene from his perch on a fire escape under a lighted bedroom, "is why them fellers both had big yeller hair ribbons on their tails, like."

"Hair ribbons!" exclaimed the Candle-Sniffer in the tone of one coming to his senses. "They wasn't no hair ribbons— Those was the toes out of my poor old mother's socks! I'd recognize them anywhere!" And with a fondly possessive tug at his radiant nose, he groaned fairly, "Can you beat it! After all these years — just as Paw always predicted she would— she's finally gone and got herself tired of bein' in the navy... But she would enlist! She would enlist!"

At that moment the truck squealed to a stop and a pig, considerably bolder and taller than its compatriots, began contentedly to munch on the unsuspecting policeman's leg.

It is far better to take an ice-cold shower any day than to sit out on the front lawn in a half tepid washboiler full of eels all making a great pretense of taking their own temperatures.

THE VERY BEST SALESMEN ARE NOT BORN

A short man chewing vigorously at a yard long alder branch was pulling his grandfather along on a green and yellow child's sled through the chief thoroughfare of Bearswah one fine morning recently. Bearswah, which had never been much more than a halfhearted waystation for stray brewers casing the lush markets to the north, was hardly even a place to live, or get older, sadder, come to no useable conclusion in, now. The hoary pullee felt this with especial keenity, for it was biting cold and, because of the jagged point of the stick, his sole remaining garment, a frayed scarlet woonsocket jacket, must perforce be left in relative safety on the towel shelf in Widder Nussmet's bathroom, where he and his younger kin had for so long made their surreptitious home.

It should be clearly stated here that their method of commercial congress— they were sheeps' bladder venders— had had a somewhat chance but nonetheless instantaneous evolvement; and that, further, at no more considerable cost than the loss of a succession of pairs of storebought teeth which, on that first as on all later occasions, had most effectually clamped themselves tightly round an old fashioned zinc chimney guard at the crown of the village's most prepossessing apartment house.

And so it was on this morning, as usual, that Senator Higgis V. Q. Vealfoot, his eyes bugging up like so many pale watery blue caps on a couple miniature quarts of frozen milk, gazed now warmly aloft at that jagged spur of the chimney guard, that mute and rusty testimonial to the surpassing goodness of (as the Senator always said it over rapturously to himself) That Damn Same Nice Big Fellow-Boy: for it must be made clear that to him it was the symbol of far more than any mere expediency of merchandizing: — *On the contrary, it was, in all truth, the actual and very real representation of the age old Answer itself;* something he could truly get his— well, anyway, get his "rottif ild froggie's behinder gooms intah."

So it is scarcely to be wondered at that, under impulse of the carefully wielded alder shoot, old Senator Higgis V. Q. Vealfoot, that stout hearted supersalesman and raconteur, surged impetuously upward... up... up... up... until he had gained to his accustomed place fast against the deeply pitted chimney guard— And oh then didn't he throw his voice proudly forth upon the cold morning air!

"Git yer sausage cases here-o, here-o, here-o, here-o! Yer nice fresh slaughtered sausage cases here-o, here-o..."

And oh is it any wonder that he paid no heed at all to doubters in the startled rooms below? Ah, yes, let them scoff all they like — "I'll hero you, you old bald bottomed reprobate!"— for the good Senator had found his chosen niche in life, and well, *ah,* how well did he know it!

A good day's hard work never hurt anybody. And especially is this true of those who make a practice of preaching this.

TAKING HOT COALS TO MISSOURI

A man in a big dusty, half-chewed hat was sitting at the bar of a honky tonk when a voice at his elbow suddenly demanded: "What are you got up in that funny rig for?"

On the point of inquiring regarding the whywithal of the stranger's unexpected interest, he turned instead to see a fellow dressed like a duck sitting right beside him. And so, he went on in a more conciliatory tone: "Whall now, partner, I be in the trade of what they call mule skinning out where I hull from."

"A mule skinner, honk?" exclaimed his new friend. "Great axe in the mornin', honk, honk! But have I got a job for you! You come right along honk with me— That damnfool wife of mine, she refuses to believe that I can turn myself into a man!"

A PASTURIZED SCENE

A little roly poly Giant Sloth chanced to be picking an bouquet of dryish blue skullcaps, when, without any warning whatever, an impetuous Cow dashed from a doorway hung with swinging bags and began at once to make wild threats against his continued safety. Much enamoured as he was by their vague, barny smell and puffy sponge-veined lips, he made in turn a most charming but nonethemore sincere gesture of offering the blossoms to her sharply divided attention. But the chuffling moocomer, who knew a sport, however natural, when she saw one, immediately thrust the poor little Giant Sloth into a nest handed her by old Bluff Durham, her ever-attentive husband, and went heelsbelling off to the market. For, you see, only the day before, while botheredly fly-ing past a shopwindow, she had noticed a pair of magnificent, shocking-pink panties, which she had every reason to believe would make her the season's most spectacular social bust.

VISIT TO A SUBURB IN HEAVEN

Tuthneda's eyes are closed, windows in a field of soft, tremblingly purple grass...

On one of the roofs a laugh clad saloon, its glasses fogged in a swirl of skirts. "This one's on me!" it calls; only to answer, "Watch it, Sugar— his wife's a pretty rough old dish of tea..." While still above that a man in a wingchair ventures a few twirling comments and, the clouds stuffed in about him more carefully, plucks up the baker's little red dog and flys off in a flurry of mounting nostalgia. Then first one building then another steps out of the graying streetscape, only to discover a tiny little princess lost asleep in its cornerstone. At which Buldy Thom, the captain of police, growls, "Ugh! just like me missus, only smaller— and a sight prettier to look at." (Just so each does one day recognize his own. For what is for one lad a toad—) Now another figure in the window above the Lobsters Club, who had been aimlessly cradling its chin in a pair of huge catsup colored pliers while watching the chorus undress in the ballrooms on its either side, breaks off as Tuthneda appears once more. For she is wonderfully enchanting! And, in fact, if the word was simply made for anybody, it was for no other but her.

A blue blue is the rain over the village. Off to the grocer's, soft basket across her flowered arm, Tuthneda trancingly goes. But not to buy any sugar sweet water biscuits or coolen of gold ale... ah no! she is only pretending to be marketing at all in order to disabuse a stern mother. And so she sings, the steeples chiming enviously in, while down the rot of shadowing wings silence leans to listen in on the unequal concert. Yet here at such a walking's end, this hut, this humble, unadorned setting— with here an empty chair, a bench unoccupied and festooned with cruel wreaths of fish lines and crab traps, and over there a table covered by an oilcloth checkered with squares of dun and darbled green. And a bed. The bed of a poor fisherman...

O as in the snowless purity of an April winter— there lies Tuthneda, in new radiance, so very prettily asleep. Ah, later... long later and then later, it will be time enough, surely more than time enough to go back through the starry mist to receive the reprimands of her unsympatico mother, who was badly shaken up in the fall of 1871*).

---

*) One of the least-publicized catastrophes of all history.

THE COCK OF ALL THE WORLD

Two olive-colored barnacle gooses waddled along the pier, complaining at being disturbed at their supper of ball-bearings and cotterkeys which they had salvaged from an accumulation of careless rollerskaters on the harbor's narrow floor. Known locally as weisswangengan, their relationship until recently had been that of mother and son. Now it would be difficult, treating of the lady first, to say which she was bigger with, guilt or egg; as for the other, foolishness seemed his most natural cover.

In her slip nearby, the *Mary Widders* was rubbing her boot-scuffed breast restlessly against *Old Jolly John,* only that morning in from Singapore, his hauser-holes still a-drip with the brackish scent of musk and untidy sandlewimps. Somewhere a man in a gay monk's cloth kimono was feeding a roll of unpunched paper into a player piano, while in the next room a well-known musical comedy composer busily cribbed down every other note; now and then, as though prodded on by an explosive clock filled with oozing milkweed, a police launch cut in and out of the jetty, leaving bits of canoes and their carefree cargoes to collect in the reddening pockets of moonlight.

And yet, *no more than a few inches in the other direction...* it was raining!

And there, people with silver bucketed heads were being tossed back and forth by two enormous children behind whom, his palely spotted tail covering the sky, a ghost-white rooster stood, negligently pecking at an unseen string of the kind packages of dust are said to come fastened with.

HOW FABLES TAPPED ALONG THE SUNKEN CORRIDORS...

I am an incorrigible believer in "Books That Change Men's Lives," and have been since Mr. Baum, Mr. Lofting, Mr. Grahame, Mr. Tolkien and forgotten others began to change mine when I was five or six. The process never ceases. In 1948 I read a pamphlet of Henry Miller's, *Patchen: Man of Anger & Light* (Padell, New York). Miller indicated that Kenneth Patchen liked Georges Rouault's work. It thus seemed reasonable I should offer Patchen the use of my one art treasure, acquired during fitful days as a Princeton undergraduate—an aquatint of Rouault's "The Yellow Clown." In early 1949 I'd left Princeton, as much for reading Miller, Patchen and Thoreau as for any reason I can now remember. I'd studied painting with Karl Knaths and gone to New York City to enroll in Stanley William Hayter's *Atelier 17* of engraving and etching. While there, a friend, also renegade from Princeton, suggested a trip to Old Lyme, Connecticut, to meet Patchen and to bestow the Rouault. So this took place one November Sunday, and it was one of those meetings you read about in the "Books That Change Men's Lives." Kenneth and Miriam Patchen lived in a tiny red cottage, about a half-mile from the Old Lyme post office. The lane led up a little hill by the township library, down past a pond full of turtles, and then to the left. The cabin sat in Connecticut less than it did in the context of many of Kenneth's love poems. All the neighborhood animals sat on the lawn like hieratic beasts. One expected some of the little green deer and the red and yellow birds of childhood. It was all a bit like Gilchrist's *Life of Blake*—Kate and Will at Felpham—a veritable enchantment. There was no "strain" for this. One simply felt it.... The visit was a brief one. Snow was falling by night and my friend and I had the trip back to New York before the highway coated over. The loan of the Rouault was graciously accepted and we left with our own various treasures—the painted books or manuscript pages or records or foods that the Patchens always bestowed so generously.

Next spring I got a letter from Miriam. Kenneth's spinal troubles had worsened considerably. They wondered if I might be free to spend a while with them in Connecticut taking dictation of a new book and preparing its typescript. I wrote back I would love to but would have to wait a few weeks because I had promised Bill Hayter to help with renovations on his Washington Street house before he left for France.

Copyright © 1970 by Jonathan Williams. The preceeding collection
was first published as *Jargon 6*.

Those were the days when even the New Haven & Hartford was pleasant to ride. I always liked the trip to Old Saybrook and the taxi ride over the Connecticut River; then the several miles through the township to the Patchens' cottage. The amosphere was much as before, albeit more so, with the cherry tree in full blossom and the grass incredibly green. Miriam had been busy painting the living room a rich cobalt blue, under the watchful eye of the huge, very silent black cat, Pushkin. Patchen himself was feeling terrible, unable to get out into the sunshine more than even once a week. His spine at that time gave him almost no flexibility. Either he stood or he lay down. Which was why writing (i.e., the mechanics of it) was nearly impossible, though he continued to think of it all the time. It is the nature of Patchen's imagination that it never sleeps, contemptuous of the obstacles of all the pain.

We established a routine of two or three hours' work, morning and afternoon, with me at the typewriter and Patchen in bed working from occasional scraps of notes but, primarily, just out of the air. As we would get into a particular fable (the book was to be a large collection of fables—his first prose in about five years, since *Panels For the Walls of Heaven*), I would read back to him what we had thus far on paper. Then he would proceed, unerringly, to dictate the tales. In some cases the initial typescript served as the basis of a rewriting; but often the text had emerged directly, fresh from that extraordinary tap Patchen has to his realm of Spirit. His ability to have these elaborate puns and names and situations so firmly in mind strikes me as no less a wonder than Frederick Delius's ability (despite blindness and paralysis) to compose via his amanuensis, Eric Fenby, so movingly described in the latter's book, *Delius As I Knew Him* (G. Bell & Sons Ltd., London, 1936) ... And so it was in the course of May, 1950, that some eighty to one hundred fables and other little tales came into being. Of the rest of the month I remember these details which had their own fabulous air: the ample delicacies Miriam provided from her mother's Finnish recipes; the books, from which I found a special favorite, David Gascoyne's *Hoelderlin's Madness,* with its beautiful italic type by Eric Gill; the watercolors by Henry Miller; the fragment of engraving from Blake's *America,* a gift from Ruthven Todd; the wonderful correspondences from Miller, from Dylan Thomas and Henri Michaux and many others; the Bunk Johnson and George Lewis records that Bill Russell was sending from Chicago. (A little later, it was these LPs that Patchen used in making private tapes of the fables. All kinds of homemade noises and jazz were interpolated back of the voice. I don't know what's become of these tapes, made by two young Patchen enthusiasts from Harvard, Alden Ashforth and David Wykoff. They were, to my knowledge, the first instances of the later poetry/jazz experiment.)

All during my visit to Old Lyme I also recall our waiting for an augury. James Laughlin was going to materialize in a seaplane (the Patchens seemed to think) at any moment and land in the Connecticut River. I never quite understood how Laughlin's 6'5" would fit into such a rig. At any rate, the plane never buzzed the red cottage and New Directions never published *Fables & Other Little Tales*. It became *Jargon #6*, my first real book as a publisher. In 1952, in the Army Medical Corps outside Stuttgart, Germany, I'd received a small legacy from the death of a close friend, Charles Neal of Demorest, Georgia. I wrote Patchen that I would use the money for publishing and that I would welcome an appropriate manuscript. *Fables,* of course, answered the demand exactly. For eight months of 1953 the book was in press at *Verlagsdruckerei Gebr. Tron, KG,* Karlsruhe-Durlach/Baden. Herr Tron was hardly a specialist in American dada, but he printed a most handsome book indeed. I read proofs and galleys during night duty in the locked N-P ward, since some of the patients were genuine paranoiacs and psychopaths, capable of attack at any instant for no particular reason. Never had Patchen's "go with it" technique, in which one thing does *not* lead to another, made more sense to me than in the hospital in Bad Cannstatt, on a hill above the Neckar. It took approximately fifty trips from Stuttgart to Karlsruhe-Durlach, some 80 kilometers, to complete the work on *Fables*. By taxi to the Bahnhof, a coffee and Kirschwasser, a croissant or a pretzel at dawn, and two hours' sleep until the suburb, Durlach.

Fables was first published October, 1953. The only review was by Robert Creeley—a very equitable one. Beyond that—nothing but the familiar Conspiracy of Silence, to use Kenneth Rexroth's phrase. A collective turning of backs and shifting of asses. Nothing very organized, simply that unionized apathy, jealous disinterest, and niggardly behavior of literary drones. It remains one of Patchen's best books—one of the few original works in this genre since Sandburg's *Rootabaga Stories*. It is, accordingly, a pleasure to have it brought back into circulation for new readers by New Directions.

JONATHAN WILLIAMS
Executive Director: The Jargon Society
Highlands, North Carolina
September 27, 1969

New Directions Paperbooks

Ilangô Adigal, *Shilappadikaram.* NDP162.
Corrado Alvaro, *Revolt in Aspromonte.* NDP119.
Guillaume Apollinaire. *Selected Writings.*† NDP310.
Djuna Barnes, *Nightwood.* NDP98.
Charles Baudelaire, *Flowers of Evil.*† NDP71.
  Paris Spleen. NDP294.
Eric Bentley, *Bernard Shaw.* NDP59.
Wolfgang Borchert, *The Man Outside.* NDP319.
Jorge Luis Borges, *Labyrinths.* NDP186.
Jean-François Bory, *Once Again.* NDP256.
Paul Bowles, *The Sheltering Sky.* NDP158.
Kay Boyle, *Thirty Stories.* NDP62.
W. Bronk, *The World, the Worldless.* NDP157.
Buddha, *The Dhammapada.* NDP188.
Louis-Ferdinand Céline, *Guignol's Band.* NDP278.
  Journey to the End of the Night. NDP84.
Blaise Cendrars, *Selected Writings.*† NDP203.
B-c. Chatterjee, *Krishnakanta's Will.* NDP120.
Jean Cocteau, *The Holy Terrors.* NDP212.
  The Infernal Machine. NDP235.
Contemporary German Poetry.†
  (Anthology) NDP148.
Hayden Carruth, *For You.* NDP298.
Cid Corman, *Livingdying.* NDP289.
  Sun Rock Man. NDP318.
Gregory Corso, *Elegiac Feelings American.* NDP299.
  Long Live Man. NDP127.
  Happy Birthday of Death. NDP86.
Edward Dahlberg, *Reader.* NDP246.
  Because I Was Flesh. NDP227.
David Daiches, *Virginia Woolf.*
  (Revised) NDP96.
Osamu Dazai, *The Setting Sun.* NDP258.
Robert Duncan, *Roots and Branches.* NDP275.
  Bending the Bow. NDP255.
Richard Eberhart, *Selected Poems.* NDP198.
Russell Edson, *The Very Thing That Happens.* NDP137.
Wm. Empson, *7 Types of Ambiguity.* NDP204.
  Some Versions of Pastoral. NDP92.
Wm. Everson, *The Residual Years.* NDP263.
Lawrence Ferlinghetti, *Her.* NDP88.
  Back Roads to Far Places. NDP312.
  A Coney Island of the Mind. NDP74.
  The Mexican Night. NDP300.
  Routines. NDP187.
  The Secret Meaning of Things. NDP268.
  Starting from San Francisco. NDP 220.
  Tyrannus Nix?. NDP288.
  Unfair Arguments with Existence. NDP143.
Ronald Firbank, *Two Novels.* NDP128.
Dudley Fitts.
  Poems from the Greek Anthology. NDP60.
F. Scott Fitzgerald, *The Crack-up.* NDP54.
Robert Fitzgerald, *Spring Shade: Poems 1931-1970.* NDP311.
Gustave Flaubert,
  The Dictionary of Accepted Ideas. NDP230.
M. K. Gandhi, *Gandhi on Non-Violence.*
  (ed. Thomas Merton) NDP197.
André Gide. *Dostoevsky.* NDP100.
Goethe, *Faust,* Part I.
  (MacIntyre translation) NDP70.
Albert J. Guerard, *Thomas Hardy.* NDP185.
Guillevic, *Selected Poems.* NDP279.
Henry Hatfield, *Goethe.* NDP136.
  Thomas Mann. (Revised Edition) NDP101
John Hawkes, *The Cannibal.* NDP123.
  The Lime Twig. NDP95.
  Second Skin. NDP146.
  The Beetle Leg. NDP239.
  The Innocent Party. NDP238.
  Lunar Landscapes. NDP274.
Hermann Hesse, *Siddhartha.* NDP65.
Edwin Honig, *García Lorca.* (Rev.) NDP102
Christopher Isherwood, *The Berlin Stories.* NDP134.
Alfred Jarry, *Ubu Roi.* NDP105.
Robinson Jeffers, *Cawdor and Medea.* NDP293.
James Joyce, *Stephen Hero.* NDP133.
Franz Kafka, *Amerika.* NDP117.
Bob Kaufman,
  Solitudes Crowded with Loneliness. NDP199.
Hugh Kenner, *Wyndham Lewis.* NDP167.
Lincoln Kirstein,
  Rhymes & More Rhymes of a Pfc. NDP202.
P. Lal, translator, *Great Sanskrit Plays.* NDP142.
Tommaso Landolfi,
  Gogol's Wife and Other Stories. NDP207.
Lautréamont, *Maldoror.* NDP207.
Denise Levertov, *O Taste and See.* NDP149.
  The Jacob's Ladder. NDP112.
  Relearning the Alphabet. NDP290.
  The Sorrow Dance. NDP222.
  With Eyes at the Back of Our Heads. NDP229.
Harry Levin, *James Joyce.* NDP87.
García Lorca, *Selected Poems.*† NDP114.
  Three Tragedies. NDP52.
  Five Plays. NDP232.
Carson McCullers, *The Member of the Wedding* (Playscript) NDP153.
Thomas Merton, *Selected Poems.* NDP85.
  Cables to the Ace. NDP252.
  Clement of Alexandria. Gift Ed. NDP173.
  Emblems of a Season of Fury. NDP140.
  Gandhi on Non-Violence. NDP197.
  The Geography of Lograire. NDP283.
  Original Child Bomb. NDP228.
  Raids on the Unspeakable. NDP276
  The Way of Chuang Tzu. NDP276.
  The Wisdom of the Desert. NDP295.
  Zen and the Birds of Appetite. NDP261.
Henri Michaux, *Selected Writings.*† NDP264.
Henry Miller, *The Air-Conditioned Nightmare.* NDP302.
  Big Sur & The Oranges of Hieronymus Bosch. NDP161.
  The Books in My Life. NDP280.
  The Colossus of Maroussi. NDP75.
  The Cosmological Eye. NDP109.
  Henry Miller on Writing. NDP151.
  The Henry Miller Reader. NDP269.
  Remember to Remember. NDP111.
  Stand Still Like the Hummingbird. NDP236.
  The Time of the Assassins. NDP 115.
  The Wisdom of the Heart. NDP94.

Y. Mishima, *Death in Midsummer.* NDP215.
   Confessions of a Mask. NDP253.
Eugenio Montale, *Selected Poems.*† NDP193.
Vladimir Nabokov, *Nikolai Gogol.* NDP78.
New Directions 17. (Anthology) NDP103.
New Directions 18. (Anthology) NDP163.
New Directions 19. (Anthology) NDP214.
New Directions 20. (Anthology) NDP248.
New Directions 21. (Anthology) NDP277.
New Directions 22. (Anthology) NDP291.
New Directions 23. (Anthology) NDP315.
Charles Olson, *Selected Writings.* NDP231.
George Oppen, *The Materials.* NDP122.
   Of Being Numerous. NDP245.
   This In Which. NDP201.
Wilfred Owen, *Collected Poems.* NDP210.
Nicanor Parra,
   Poems and Antipoems.† NDP242.
Boris Pasternak, *Safe Conduct.* NDP77.
Kenneth Patchen, *Aflame and Afun of*
   Walking Faces. NDP292.
   Because It Is. NDP83.
   But Even So. NDP265.
   Collected Poems. NDP284.
   Doubleheader. NDP211.
   Hallelujah Anyway. NDP219.
   The Journal of Albion Moonlight. NDP99.
   Memoirs of a Shy Pornographer. NDP205.
   Selected Poems. NDP160.
   Sleepers Awake. NDP286.
   Wonderings. NDP320.
Octavio Paz, *Configurations.*† NDP303.
Plays for a New Theater. (Anth.) NDP216.
Ezra Pound, *ABC of Reading.* NDP89.
   Classic Noh Theatre of Japan. NDP79.
   The Confucian Odes. NDP81.
   Confucius. NDP285.
   Confucius to Cummings. (Anth) NDP126.
   Guide to Kulchur. NDP257.
   Literary Essays. NDP250.
   Love Poems of Ancient Egypt. Gift Edition.
     NDP178.
   Pound/Joyce. NDP296.
   Selected Cantos. NDP304.
   Selected Letters 1907-1941. NDP317.
   Selected Poems. NDP66
   The Spirit of Romance. NDP266.
   Translations.† (Enlarged Edition) NDP145.
Omar Pound, *Arabic and Persian Poems.*
   NDP305.
Raymond Queneau, *The Bark Tree.* NDP314.
Carl Rakosi, *Amulet.* NDP234.
Raja Rao, *Kanthapura.* NDP224.
Herbert Read, *The Green Child.* NDP208.
Jesse Reichek, *Etcetera.* NDP196.
Kenneth Rexroth, *Assays.* NDP113.
   An Autobiographical Novel. NDP281.
   Bird in the Bush. NDP80
   Collected Longer Poems. NDP309.
   Collected Shorter Poems. NDP243.
   Love and the Turning Year. NDP308.
   100 Poems from the Chinese. NDP192.
   100 Poems from the Japanese.† NDP147.

Charles Reznikoff, *By the Waters of Manhattan.*
   NDP121.
   Testimony: The United States 1885-1890.
     NDP200.
Arthur Rimbaud, *Illuminations.*† NDP56.
   Season in Hell & Drunken Boat.† NDP97.
Saikaku Ihara, *The Life of an Amorous*
   Woman. NDP270.
Jean-Paul Sartre, *Baudelaire.* NDP233.
   Nausea. NDP82.
   The Wall (Intimacy). NDP272.
Delmore Schwartz, *Selected Poems.* NDP241.
Stevie Smith, *Selected Poems.* NDP159.
Gary Snyder, *The Back Country.* NDP249.
   Earth House Hold. NDP267.
   Regarding Wave. NDP306.
Enid Starkie, *Arthur Rimbaud.* NDP254.
Stendhal, *Lucien Leuwen.*
   Book I: *The Green Huntsman.* NDP107.
   Book II: *The Telegraph.* NDP108.
Jules Supervielle, *Selected Writings.*† NDP209.
Dylan Thomas, *Adventures in the Skin Trade.*
   NDP183.
   A Child's Christmas in Wales. Gift Edition.
     NDP181.
   Collected Poems 1934-1952. NDP316.
   The Doctor and the Devils. NDP297.
   Portrait of the Artist as a Young Dog.
     NDP51.
   Quite Early One Morning. NDP90.
   Under Milk Wood. NDP73.
Lionel Trilling, *E. M. Forster.* NDP189.
Martin Turnell, *Art of French Fiction.* NDP251.
Paul Valéry, *Selected Writings.*† NDP184
Vernon Watkins, *Selected Poems.* NDP221.
Nathanael West, *Miss Lonelyhearts &*
   Day of the Locust. NDP125.
George F. Whicher, tr.,
   The Goliard Poets.† NDP206.
J. Willett, *Theatre of Bertolt Brecht.* NDP244.
Tennessee Williams, *Hard Candy,* NDP225.
   Camino Real. NDP301.
   Dragon Country. NDP287.
   The Glass Menagerie. NDP218.
   In the Winter of Cities. NDP154.
   One Arm & Other Stories. NDP237.
   The Roman Spring of Mrs. Stone. NDP271.
   27 Wagons Full of Cotton. NDP217.
William Carlos Williams,
   The William Carlos Williams Reader.
     NDP282.
   The Autobiography. NDP223.
   The Build-up. NDP259.
   The Farmers' Daughters. NDP106.
   In the American Grain. NDP53.
   In the Money. NDP240.
   Many Loves. NDP191.
   Paterson. Complete. NDP152.
   Pictures from Brueghel. NDP118.
   The Selected Essays. NDP273.
   Selected Poems. NDP131.
   A Voyage to Pagany. NDP307.
   White Mule. NDP226.
John D. Yohannan,
   Joseph and Potiphar's Wife. NDP262.

Complete descriptive catalog available free on request from
New Directions, 333 Sixth Avenue, New York 10014. † Bilingual.